To Jesse—
Always keep your
heart smiling!
Keri A Gonzálery

May all of your
dreams come true!!
Debbie Moldovan ♡

A Glove of Their Own

Written by
Debbie Moldovan, Keri Conkling
and Lisa Funari-Willever

Illustrated by
Lauren Lambiase

FM
FRANKLIN MASON PRESS

Trenton, New Jersey

Text copyright 2008 © Debbie Moldovan, Keri Conkling, Lisa Funari-Willever

Illustration Copyright 2008 © Lauren Lambiase

Cover and Interior Design by Peri Poloni-Gabriel,
Knockout Design, Naperville, IL – www.knockoutbooks.com

Editorial Staff: Marcia Jacobs, Faustiene Smith, Mary Sullivan

Franklin Mason Press – ISBN No. 978-0-9760469-5-0

Library of Congress Control Number: 2008906012

Franklin Mason Press is proud to support the organizations that make a difference in
the lives of children. In that spirit, we are pleased to donate $0.10 from the sale of each
book, to each of the following organizations: Good Sports, Sports Gift, and Pitch In For
Baseball. To learn more about their work, please see our Join the Team page at the end of
the book or visit www.franklinmasonpress.com.

Published in the United States – Printed in Singapore

*For Rob, your love of baseball and desire to see every kid
have a glove of their own inspired the writing of this book!
And for my children, Tyler, Austin, and Cayla –
remember, no dream is too big!* —DM

*To my parents who taught me how to give and receive love,
my husband, Bill, my dream and my reality,
and Holly and Will, the sunshine of my life…* —KC

*And to Bob Salomon – thank you for seeking
the good left in the world. You are a dream-maker,
even for the grown-ups!* —DM and KC

*To my husband, Todd, and my three little sluggers,
Jessica, Patrick, and Timothy* —LFW

*For my dad, who taught me how to draw
and to keep my eye on the ball* —LL

Special thanks to:

*Lindsey Naber and Rawlings…true All-Stars. Your belief in and support
of this project have made a huge difference and will benefit children all over.
Delinda Lombardo and Athlebrities...thank you for your tireless efforts to
spread the news about athletes and their charitable causes.*

*The editors at Franklin Mason Press would like to thank those who
graciously serve on the Guest Young Author and Illustrator Committees.
Your care in selecting the work of young writers and artists today will
help shape and inspire the authors and illustrators of tomorrow.*

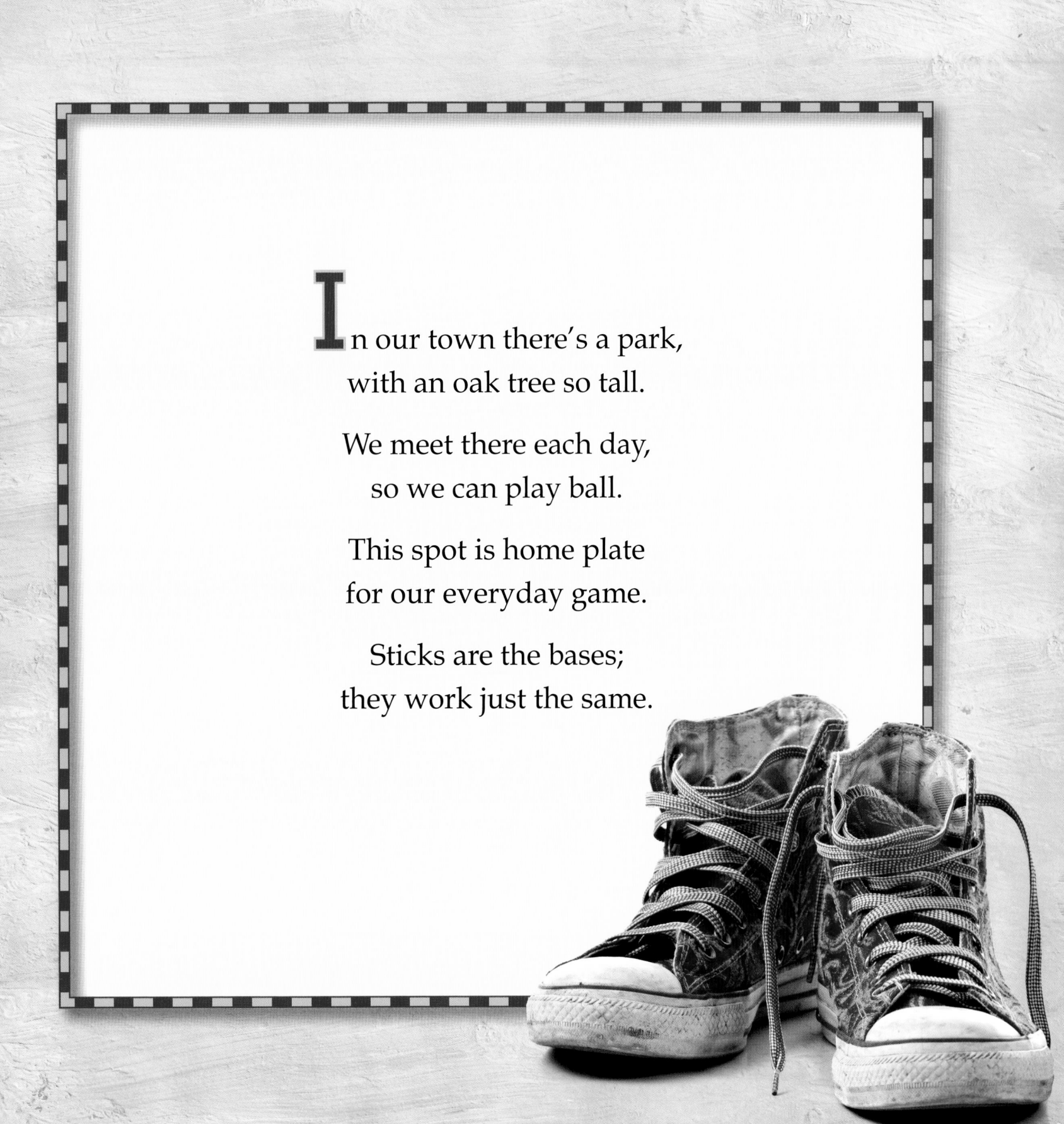

In our town there's a park,
with an oak tree so tall.

We meet there each day,
so we can play ball.

This spot is home plate
for our everyday game.

Sticks are the bases;
they work just the same.

We made up two teams on this hot summer day,

then we took to the field, so excited to play.

I grabbed the old bat and held it so tight,

knowing a base hit would start the game right.

The pitcher was ready and hollered "Let's go!"

So I lifted my heel and dug in my toe.

The first pitch was good, strike one was the call

and I heard my team yell, "Keep your eye on the ball."

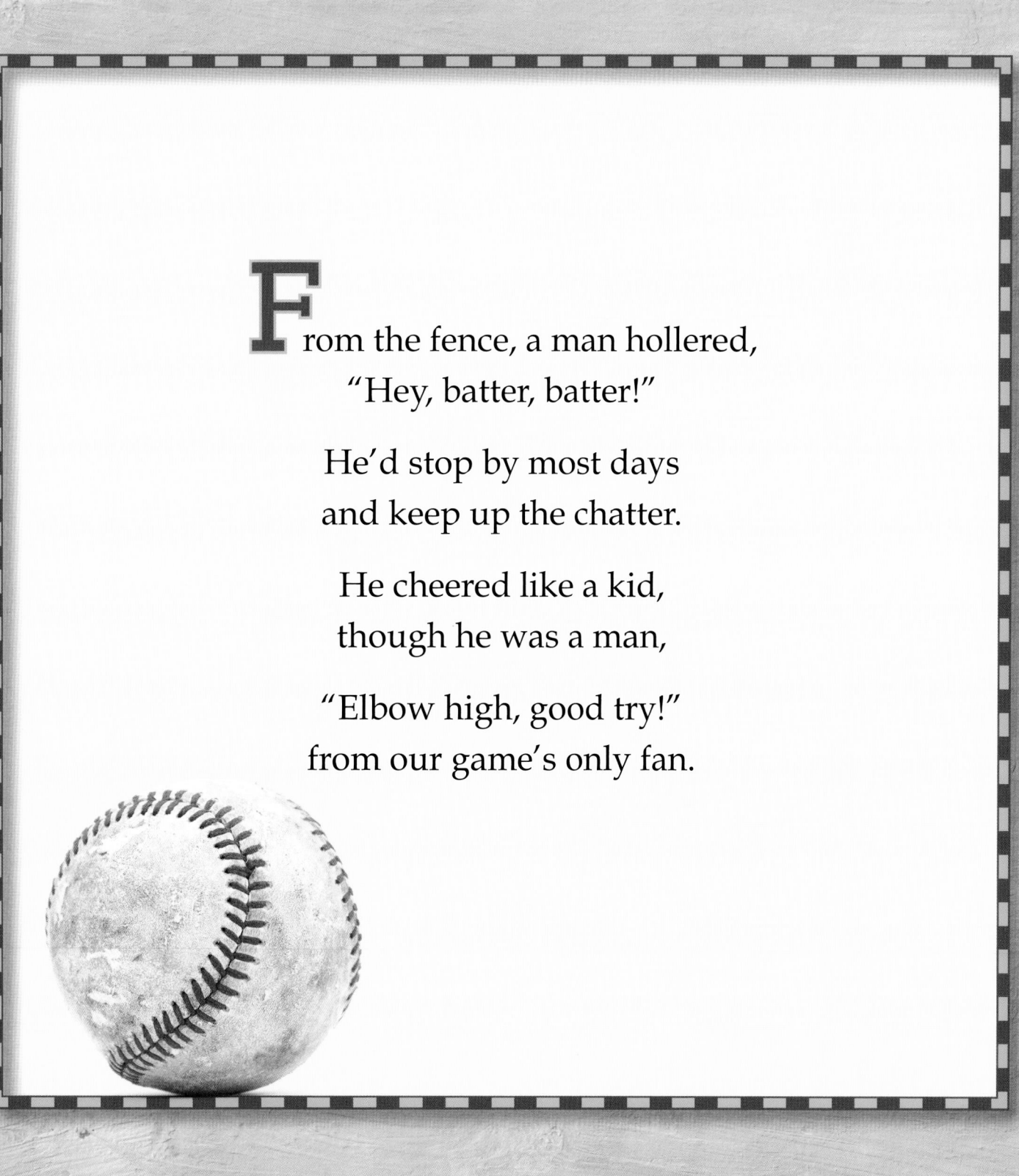

From the fence, a man hollered,
"Hey, batter, batter!"

He'd stop by most days
and keep up the chatter.

He cheered like a kid,
though he was a man,

"Elbow high, good try!"
from our game's only fan.

I took a deep breath, choked up and held tight,

but the second pitch sailed by then sunk to the right.

I was down in the count and I needed a hit.

The pitcher looked left and pounded his mitt.

I imagined fans cheering and nothing was sweeter.

In my mind, it's the playoffs, so bring on the heater!

I could picture the stands and the centerfield wall.

As the pitcher wound up, I stared down the ball.

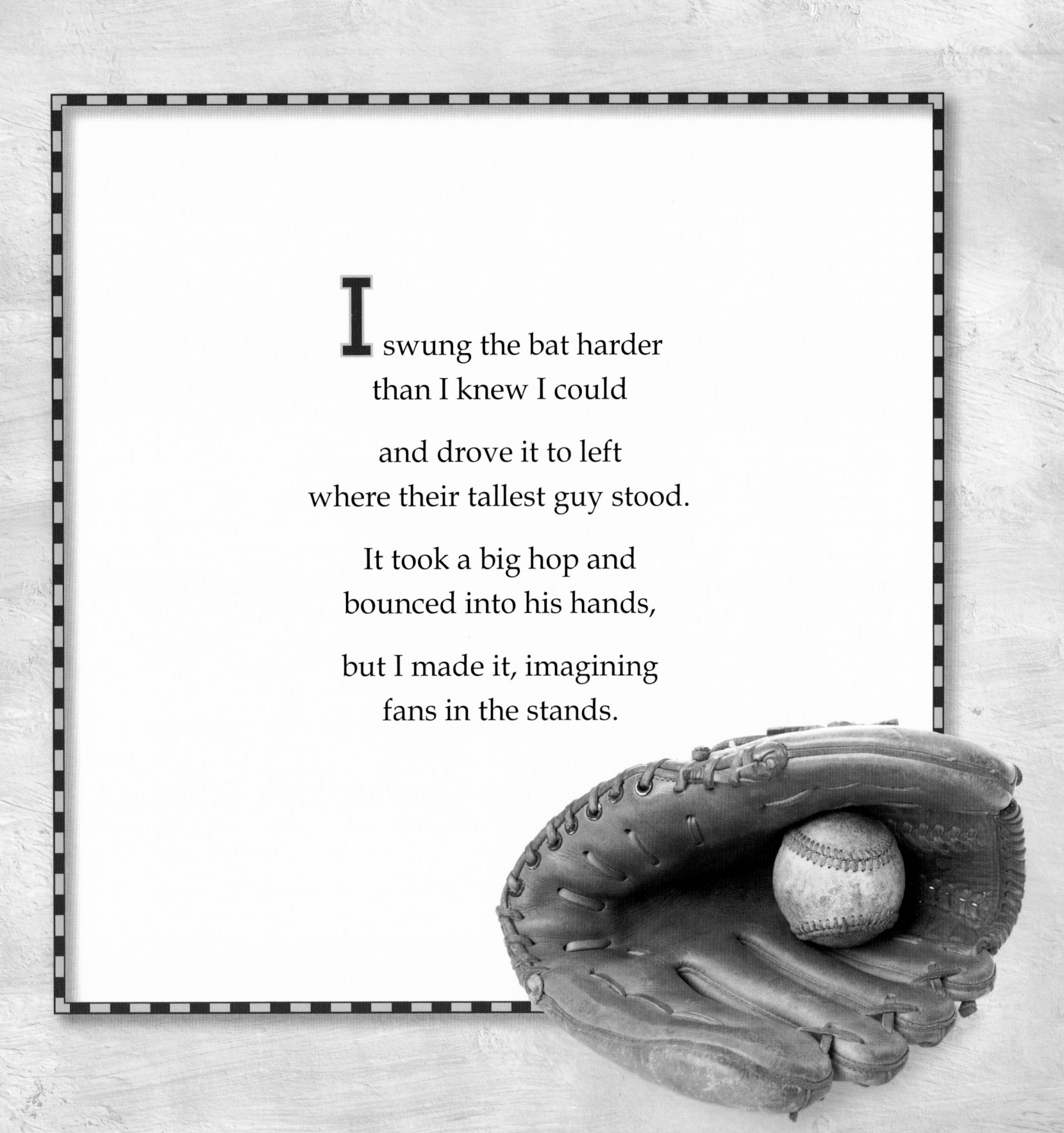

I swung the bat harder
than I knew I could

and drove it to left
where their tallest guy stood.

It took a big hop and
bounced into his hands,

but I made it, imagining
fans in the stands.

The next batter up grabbed our worn out old bat,

took two practice swings and adjusted his hat.

A line drive to right, hit hard and hit fast,

to a fielder with no mitt to catch this quick blast.

Despite stinging hands, he torpedoed the ball

and despite my hard running, "You're out," was the call.

Then a quick throw to first, a double play made.

Now, *this* was excitement, *the reason* we played!

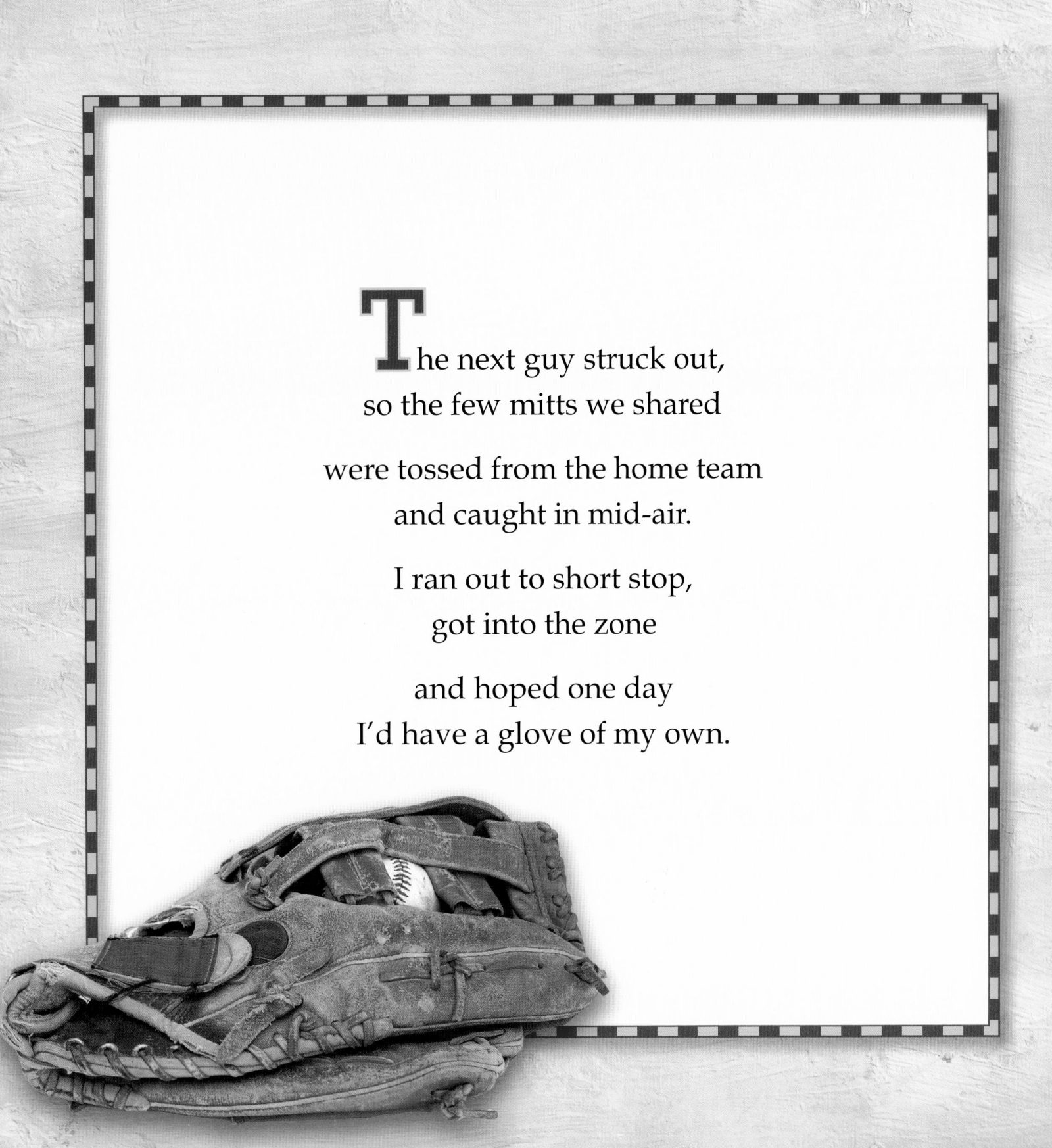

The next guy struck out,
so the few mitts we shared

were tossed from the home team
and caught in mid-air.

I ran out to short stop,
got into the zone

and hoped one day
I'd have a glove of my own.

P laying each day, like the other kids do,

except we wished for things that would never come true.

The little we had was so worn out and old,

that a new bat or new cleats were worth more than gold.

With no bleachers, no benches, no scoreboard to use,

rocks kept the score and we played in old shoes.

But for us, it was more than just innings and outs.

Dreams on a field, that's what this was about.

Then one day, that man
from the fence, I could see,

was pulling big bags
by the big home plate tree.

He smiled and said when
his own kids were small,

this was the same place
that they would play ball.

"My kids are now grown," said our number one fan,

in fact, my son's son is almost a man.

But I found these old bags, in the strangest of places

and thought of your field and the sticks used for bases.

"I once was a coach, so there's old mitts and bats,

some shirts, and some balls, and even some hats.

And two dozen cleats, in all different sizes. Enjoy!"

said our fan who was full of surprises.

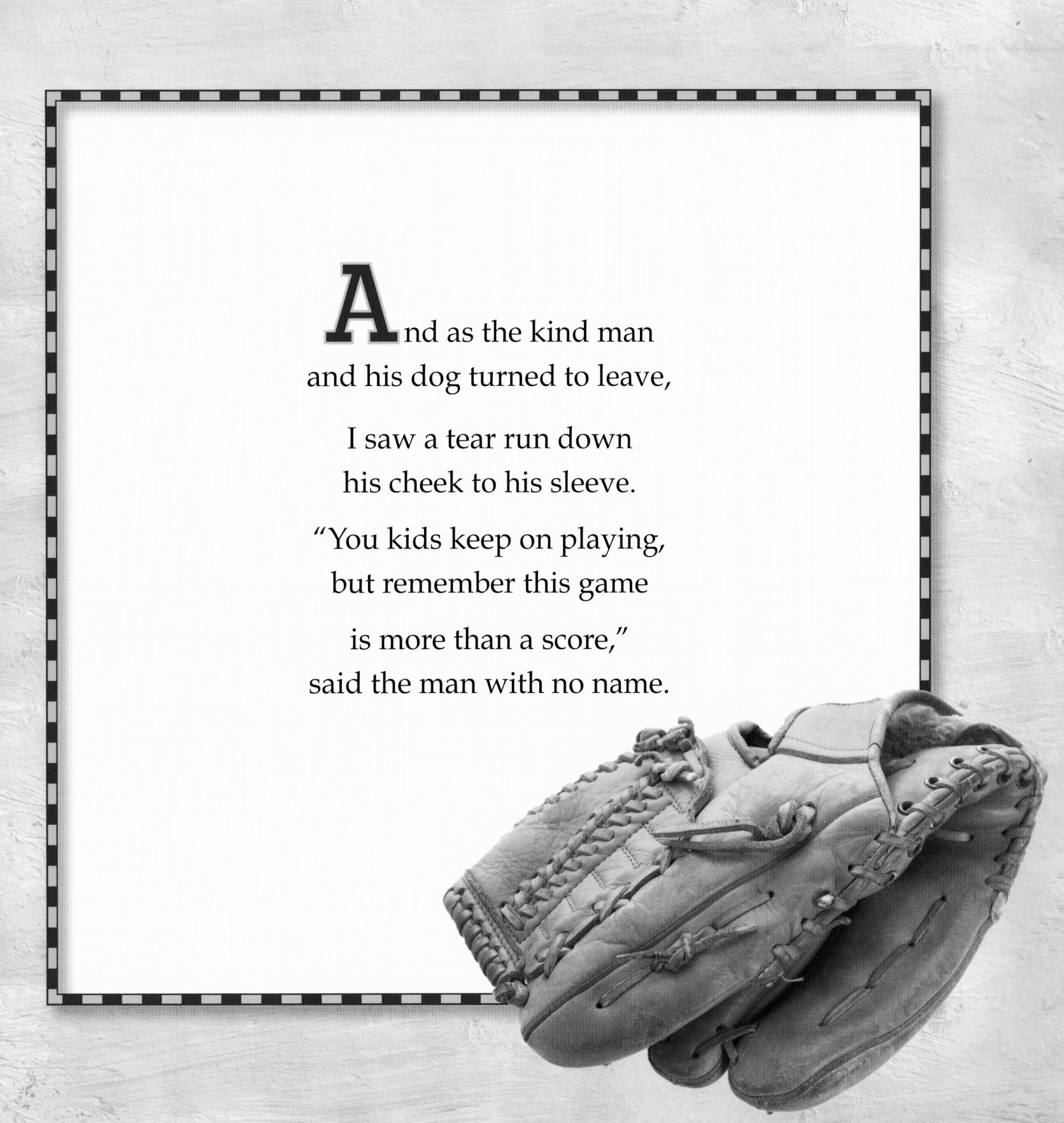

And as the kind man
and his dog turned to leave,

I saw a tear run down
his cheek to his sleeve.

"You kids keep on playing,
but remember this game

is more than a score,"
said the man with no name.

So to honor that man by the fence with no name

we decided that one day we'd each do the same.

We treasured those old gloves, each bat and each ball

and one day *we'll* place them in hands big and small.

For few things in life are ever as good,

as the smell of your own glove, the crack of the wood.

Or being with friends, at that one special spot

and sharing what you have…. *with those who have not.*

Meet the Coach & Fans

Franklin Mason Press is proud to have worked with a fantastic team in creating *A Glove of Their Own* and we are thrilled to become a part of the - *playing the game forward* ideal. We hope that this story moves everyone to join the team and ensure all kids have *a glove of their own*. So many talented, creative people and organizations have already joined the team, but one member of the team deserves special recognition…

COACH BOB SALOMON

As a lifelong fan of baseball, coach, and father of Daniel and Julia, Bob has helped turn *A Glove of Their Own* into more than a book, but a movement. This story is for the kids who toss the bat to choose captains and pick teams, playing in a neighborhood field or an empty lot. You'll find no coaches, no concession stands, and sometimes just an old bat and ball. But once the first pitch is thrown, you'll find the real heart and soul of America. You'll find baseball in its purest form. And if you look a little closer, you'll find something more.

The story of donating equipment to kids who would otherwise go without is not fiction. It happens every day with companies, large and small, whose main goal is to place this equipment in the hands of children. Bob believes in the positive effects of teamwork, sportsmanship, and lending a hand. With the support of Rawlings, Louisville Slugger, and Modell's and by partnering with organizations like Good Sports, Pitch In For Baseball, and Sports Gift, he is raising awareness and financial support for this cause.

Bob and his wife, Martha, founded Danjulie Associates to rally corporations, organizations, and sports lovers and he needs your help. Join the movement that believes in the value of sportsmanship, teamwork, and getting kids back outside and into the game. To learn how you can get into the game or have this book become a part of your organization's fund-raising efforts, visit www.agloveoftheirown.com or e-mail agototellus@aol.com.

PLAYING THE GAME…FORWARD!

Special thanks to our many fans and supporters:

Rawlings

Louisville Slugger

Modell's Sporting Goods

Good Sports

Pitch In For Baseball

Sports Gift

Make-A-Wish Foundation® of New Jersey

Sunshine Foundation

Athlebrities

Lakewood Blue Claws
Minor League Baseball Team

Look To The Stars

K.I.D.S. (Kids in Distressed Situations)

Cheerful Givers

And our professional baseball players and agents:

Craig Biggio

Sean Casey

Jack Hannahan

Robb Quinlan

Joe Speed

Join the Team

The following organizations make the dreams of children come true and Franklin Mason Press has selected them to be our designated partner charities for this book. Ten cents from the sale of each book is automatically donated to each group and when each organization sells books through their membership or fund-raisers we are pleased to donate $3.00 per book. We are also honored to provide space in our book to share their touching messages with our readers. Through their determination and creativity, they provide equipment to children who would otherwise go without. Whether they collect and re-distribute used equipment or solicit donations from generous individuals and corporations to provide new equipment, they touch the lives of our future. We invite you to visit their websites and join the team!

GOOD SPORTS

In the past five years, Good Sports has helped thousands of kids score more goals, catch more fly balls and celebrate more victories than ever before.

But any player knows, it's not just about winning. It's about being in the game. Because kids who play sports don't just benefit physically – they also develop confidence, self-worth and valuable skills like teamwork. All payoffs that last a lifetime. Due to economic realities, there are many young people who don't have the chance to get in the game. The costs of participating are on the rise, and program budgets are being cut nationwide, leaving a lot of kids on the sidelines.

That's where Good Sports comes in to play. Five years ago, we started with the simple goal of helping more disadvantaged kids get access to sports equipment. Since then, we've provided more than $3.1 million worth of gear and impacted over 150,000 young people. We've helped more than 520 community organizations both add programs and reduce the costs of participation. And we've donated equipment for everything from football and baseball to tennis, hockey and sailing.

And we're getting stronger every year. Since our first program in 2003, we've expanded our reach from Boston to Providence, Philadelphia and Chicago, with more cities on the horizon. Thanks to our funding partners, equipment manufacturers and, especially, people like you, we've made every dollar go the distance, getting $2 worth of equipment for every $1 donation we receive.

That means a lot of baseball gloves, jerseys and ice skates where there were none before. And that means a lot more kids on the field, on the rink and in the game.

Good Sports strives to provide the same opportunity you read about in *A Glove of Their Own* to children all over the country. Thank you for your support of this book and the thousands of young people it represents. To get involved or learn more about Good Sports visit us at www.goodsports.org.

PITCH IN FOR BASEBALL

Pitch In For Baseball® is a 501 c 3 charitable organization headquartered outside of Philadelphia, Pennsylvania. The mission of Pitch In For Baseball (www.pitchinforbaseball.org) is to improve the social, emotional and physical well being of children in need through the game of baseball. Since 2005, it has collected and redistributed baseball and softball equipment and uniforms to underserved children in over 50 countries around the world and more than 100 communities in the United States. You can contact Pitch In For Baseball Executive Director David Rhode at drhode@pitchinforbaseball.org or at 215-371-2841.

"Let your equipment play extra innings!"

SPORTS GIFT

The charity Sports Gift provides sports equipment to help underprivileged children all over the world play sports. If you want to donate your old sports equipment to Sports Gift, please mail your donations to their address below. If you would like to organize a collection of sports equipment in your community to send to Sports Gift, please contact Sports Gift for more information on their Collection Leader community service program.

SPORTS GIFT
32545 B Golden Lantern, #478
Dana Point, CA, USA 92629
Phone: 949.388.2359
Email: sportsgift@cox.net
Website: www.sportsgift.org

Guest Young Author

1st

REBECA FAGAN

Age 7, Pompton Lakes, New Jersey,
Our Lady of Consolation Academy

THE BUNNY WHO HAD A FLOWER

One day a bunny walked by a garden. The garden had lots of flowers because it was spring. There were all different colored flowers. The bunny picked one of the red flowers. It was a rose. This rose was beautiful. The bunny said he would keep the rose safe forever.

One day the bunny lost the rose and he was very sad. He looked for the rose everywhere, but he couldn't find it. So he decided to make his own garden. He planted all sorts of flowers in his garden, but no red roses. He kept it nice and neat and pulled out the weeds. He watered the flowers everyday to make it the most beautiful garden ever. But he still missed his red rose.

A few days later, he came outside and saw that all of his flowers were gone. He was so upset. When he looked again, he noticed one flower in the garden. It was his red rose, the most beautiful rose he had ever seen. Even though all of his other flowers were gone, he had his red rose back and he was very, very happy.

2nd

CHELSEA CONSOLINI

Age 8, River Vale, New Jersey,
Woodside Elementary School

SUPERSAURUS

Once there was a Supersaurus named Super. He always liked to eat plants all day. His friends were also plant-eaters and played with him a lot. One day they were playing by trees and a bunch of meat-eaters came up behind them. Super whipped his tail at the Allosaurus but it didn't work. The Tyrannosaurus Rex said, "Want to fight?" in a creepy voice. His friends said, "No," but Super said, "Yes." So they started to fight. Super was trying wrap him with his long neck and the Tyrannosaurus Rex was trying to knock him down. Then Super had an idea. He said, "Hey, there's a bunch of little dinosaurs you can eat. The Tyrannosaurus Rex looked and Super knocked him into a tree. And that was the end of the meat-eaters because they ran away in fear.

3rd

KAITLYN RIGGIO

Age 8, East Windsor, New Jersey,
Grace N. Rogers School

I DON'T WANT TO BE A PENCIL

Kaitlyn did not like being short, but one thing was for sure – she did not want to be a pencil. It was a spring day and Kaitlyn was going outside to play. She picked up a jump rope for her and her friends to play with. As they lined up to play limbo, Kaitlyn noticed that only Rachel was shorter than her. Kaitlyn was sad and went to her room and talked to herself out loud. To her surprise, she got an answer and it was from her pencil. "Well, you don't want to be a pencil," said the pencil. "You write with me all day and what do I get? I go in that thing and get my bottom chopped off." Kaitlyn thought about and even though she did not like being small, one thing was for sure…she didn't ever want to be a pencil.

Guest Young Illustrator

1st

JOSEPH TICE
Age 9, Belford, New Jersey,
Bayview Elementary School

"WELCOME TO EARTH"

2nd

SEBASTIAN PATIN
Age 9,
Belford, New Jersey,
Bayview Elementary School

"PARADISE"

3rd

RIANA RIDDICK
Age 8,
Manahawkin, New Jersey,
Ocean Acres Elementary School

"BE CAREFUL WHERE YOU SWIM"

FRANKLIN MASON PRESS is looking for stories and illustrations from kids 6-9 years old to appear in our books. We are dedicated to providing children with an avenue into the world of publishing. If you would like to be our next Guest Young Author or Guest Young Illustrator, send us your work. Be sure to follow the rules listed at our website, www.franklinmasonpress.com.

TO BE A GUEST YOUNG AUTHOR:
Send us a 75-200 word story about something strange, funny, or unusual. Stories may be fiction and non-fiction.

TO BE A GUEST YOUNG ILLUSTRATOR:
Draw a picture using crayons, markers, or colored pencils. Do not write words on your picture.

PRIZES
1st Place Author/1st Place Illustrator
$25.00, a framed award, a complimentary book and your work will be published in FMP's newest book.

2nd Place Author/2nd Place Illustrator
$15.00, a framed award, a complimentary book and your work will be published in FMP's newest book.

3rd Place Author/3rd Place Illustrator
$10.00, a framed award, a complimentary book and your work will be published in FMP's newest book.

For complete rules and information, visit www.franklinmasonpress.com

About the Authors and Illustrator

DEBBIE MOLDOVAN, *Author*

Debbie was raised in New Hyde Park, New York. She attended Hofstra University where she earned a B.B.A. in Marketing and a M.S. in Elementary Education. She resides in Basking Ridge, New Jersey with her husband, Rob and their three children, Tyler, Austin and Cayla. She has taught first grade and computers and is currently teaching preschool in Basking Ridge while following her life long dream of writing children's books. She is actively involved in her children's schools, volunteers her time to support local athletic programs, as well as several charities which are of importance to her and her family.

KERI CONKLING, *Author*

Keri was raised in Pequannock, New Jersey where her passion for reading and writing led her to major in English while attending Montclair State University. After graduating, it was her desire to help others which led her to a career in Human Resources. Keri is married to her childhood sweetheart, Bill, and resides in Basking Ridge, New Jersey. They share their life, love of family, passion for education, and volunteerism with their two children, Holly and Will.

LISA FUNARI-WILLEVER, *Author*

Lisa, a native of Trenton, New Jersey and now residing in Columbus, New Jersey, is the author of 16 books for children and teachers. Married to Todd Willever, a captain in the Trenton Fire Department, they have three children, Jessica, Patrick, and Timothy and they are adopting a little girl from Moldova. A graduate of Trenton State College and former teacher, she loves nothing more than traveling with her family and visiting schools all over the world.

LAUREN LAMBIASE, *Illustrator*

Lauren's dream has always been to follow in her father's footsteps and become a professional illustrator. She recently completed four years at the University of the Arts in Philadelphia and is currently taking her first big step into the world of publishing. By the summer of 2008, her detailed and realistic oil paintings will fill the pages of her first illustrated children's book, *A Glove of Their Own*. To view her work, visit www.LaurenLambiase.com.

About Franklin Mason Press

Franklin Mason Press was founded in Trenton, New Jersey in September 1999. While our main goal is to produce quality books, we also provide children with an avenue into the world of publishing. Our Guest Young Author and Illustrator Contest offers children an opportunity to submit their work and possibly become published authors and illustrators. In addition, Franklin Mason Press is proud to support children's charities with donations from each book sold and space in our books to share their messages with our young readers, their families and their schools. Each new children's title benefits a children's charity.

For more information, please visit
www.franklinmasonpress.com

Franklin Mason Press
PO Box 3808, Trenton, New Jersey 08629